MINI CLASSICS

PUSS IN BOOTS

A Parragon Book

Published by
Parragon Books,
Unit 13–17, Avonbridge Trading Estate,
Atlantic Road, Avonmouth, Bristol BS11 9QD.

Produced by
The Templar Company plc,
Pippbrook Mill, London Road, Dorking, Surrey RH4 1JE.

Designed by Mark Kingsley-Monks

Printed and bound in Great Britain

ISBN 1-85813-620-2

MINI CLASSICS

PUSS IN BOOTS

RETOLD BY STEPHANIE LASLETT
ILLUSTRATED BY DAVID ANSTEY

There was once an old miller who had three sons. After some time, the miller fell ill and when he knew he was about to die, he called in his sons and divided his

property between them.
He did not own much and
so the deed was soon done.
To his eldest son he gave
his mill, to his second
son he gave his donkey
and to his youngest son
he gave his cat.

Now the youngest son
was very unhappy to be
left such a small share
of his father's belongings.

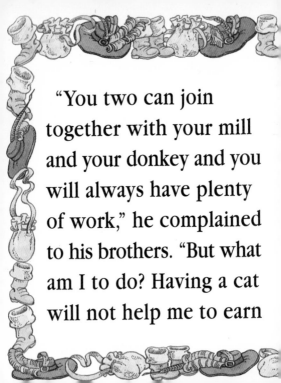

"You two can join together with your mill and your donkey and you will always have plenty of work," he complained to his brothers. "But what am I to do? Having a cat will not help me to earn money. All he is good for is catching mice. Now I will surely starve to death!"

Now the cat heard all this, and spoke to the youngest son in a grave and serious voice.

"Do not worry, my good master. All you have to do is give me a bag, and get a pair of boots made for me, so I may scamper through the dirt and the brambles,

and you will soon see
that you have got the
best part of your father's
belongings."

But the cat's master did not build his hopes too high. After all, a cat dressed in boots and carrying a bag is still only a cat. But then he remembered seeing Puss play a great many

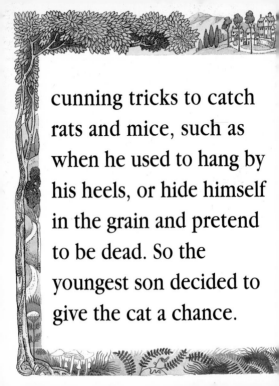

cunning tricks to catch rats and mice, such as when he used to hang by his heels, or hide himself in the grain and pretend to be dead. So the youngest son decided to give the cat a chance.

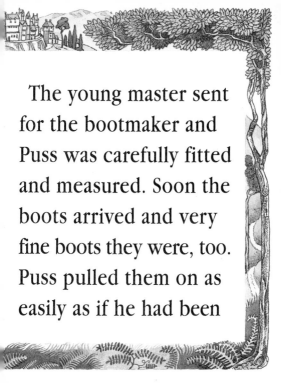

The young master sent for the bootmaker and Puss was carefully fitted and measured. Soon the boots arrived and very fine boots they were, too. Puss pulled them on as easily as if he had been

wearing them all his life.
A smart hat and a stout
bag were also found for
him and the first thing
Puss did was to stuff the
bag with bran and thistles.
Then he tiptoed into the
rabbit warren, stretched

out upon the ground
and, holding the string
of the bag in his paws, he
pretended to be dead.

Now older, more experienced rabbits would not fall for such a trick, but Puss lay quietly and hoped that the younger bunnies might be tempted by the tasty titbits inside his bag.

21

Soon, after much sniffing and nibbling, he had what he wanted. A rash and foolish young rabbit jumped right into the bag, and Master Puss quickly drew the strings tight! The poor rabbit

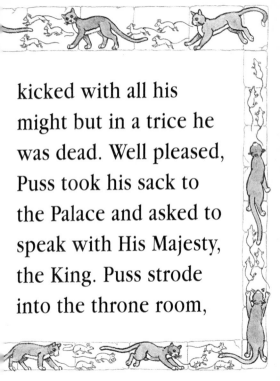

kicked with all his
might but in a trice he
was dead. Well pleased,
Puss took his sack to
the Palace and asked to
speak with His Majesty,
the King. Puss strode
into the throne room,

bowed low and said:
"Sir, I have brought
you a rabbit — a gift
from my noble Lord, the
Marquis of Carabas,"
(for that was the new
title which Puss had
made up for his Master).

"We hope your Royal
Majesty will enjoy it."

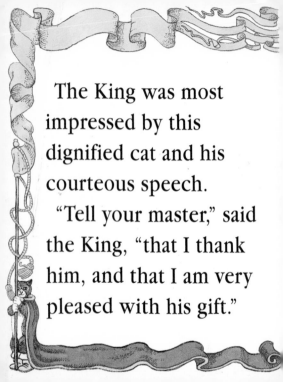

The King was most impressed by this dignified cat and his courteous speech.

"Tell your master," said the King, "that I thank him, and that I am very pleased with his gift."

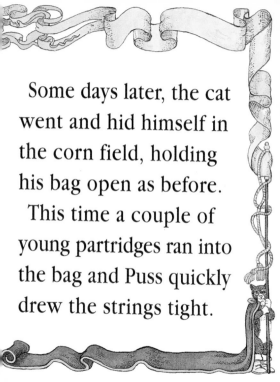

Some days later, the cat went and hid himself in the corn field, holding his bag open as before.

This time a couple of young partridges ran into the bag and Puss quickly drew the strings tight.

Once again the cat
visited the Palace and,
with a twirl of his
whiskers, he presented
his catch to the King.-

"From my noble Lord,
the Marquis of Carabas,"
he explained.

29

The King received the partridges with great pleasure, and ordered the cat to be served the Palace's finest wine.

The next time Puss ventured out hunting, he caught a brace of

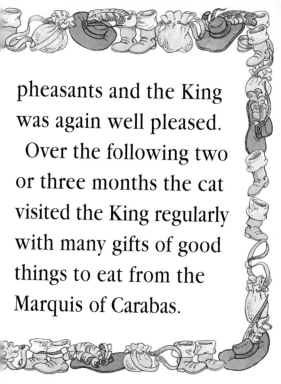

pheasants and the King was again well pleased.

Over the following two or three months the cat visited the King regularly with many gifts of good things to eat from the Marquis of Carabas.